TO SUE, MICHAEL, AND THE BRIGHT 1993 AUGUST AT 'LA CASA DEL PINO'

MY MAP BOOK
COPYRIGHT © 1995 BY SARA FANELLI
FIRST PUBLISHED IN 1995 BY ABC, ALL BOOKS FOR CHILDREN,
A DIVISION OF THE ALL CHILDREN'S COMPANY, LTD.
33 MUSEUM STREET, LONDON WC1A 1LD, ENGLAND
PRINTED IN SINGAPORE. ALL RIGHTS RESERVED.

LIBRARY OF CONGRESS CATALOGING-IN-PUBLICATION DATA
FANELLI, SARA.
   MY MAP BOOK / BY SARA FANELLI.
      P.   CM.
   SUMMARY: A COLLECTION OF MAPS PROVIDES VIEWS OF THE OWNER'S
BEDROOM, SCHOOL, PLAYGROUND, AND OTHER REALMS FARTHER AWAY.
   ISBN 0-06-026455-1. — ISBN 0-06-026456-X (LIB. BDG.)
   [1. MAPS - FICTION.] I. TITLE.
PZ7.F2213 MY   1995   94-48834
[E] — DC 20   CIP
                                                     AC

1 2 3 4 5 6 7 8 9 10
FIRST AMERICAN EDITION, 1995

MY MAP BOOK

SARA FANELLI

HarperCollins*Publishers*

TREES

3

1.

2.

3

THE POND

GREEN FIELD

?

THE FOREST

1

MONSTERS 2

(GUARDIANS OF THE TREASURE)

VILLAGE

X

X

DANGER!

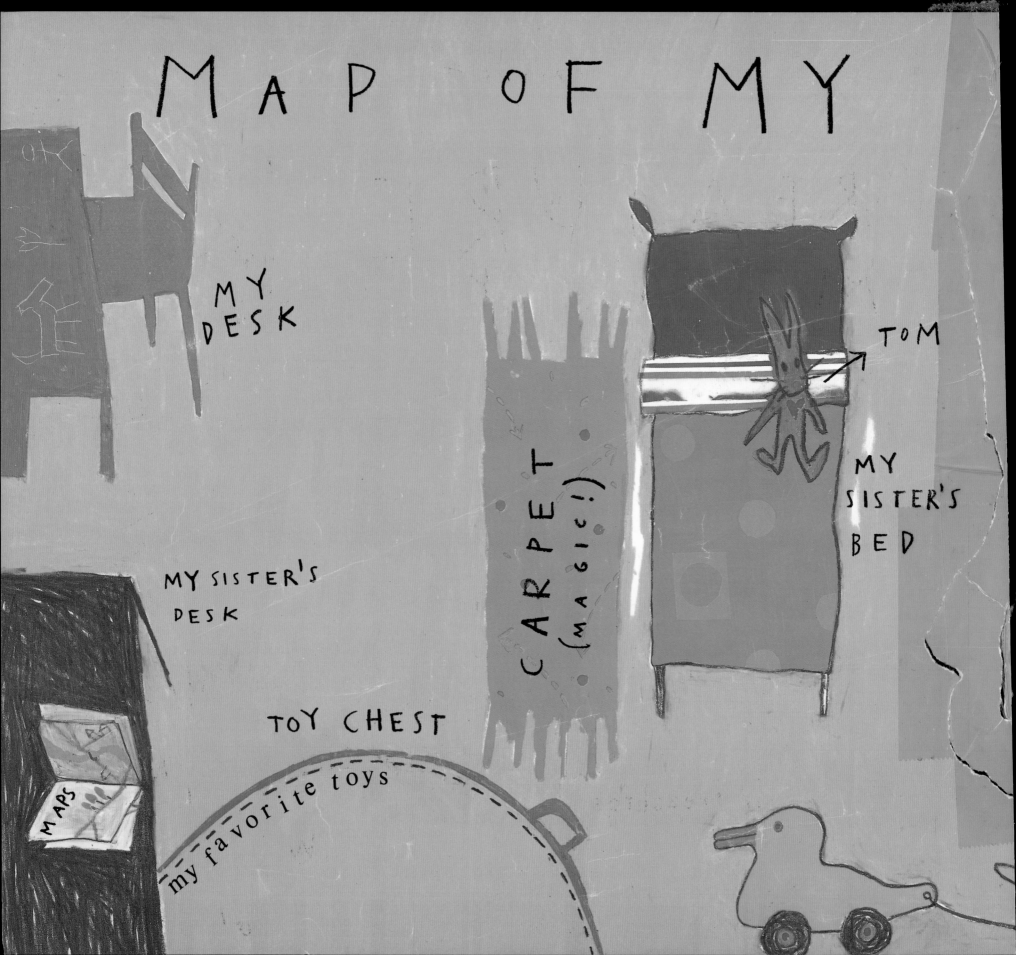

MAP OF MY

MY
DESK

MY SISTER'S
DESK

TOY CHEST

my favorite toys

MAPS

CARPET
(magic!)

TOM

MY
SISTER'S
BED

MAP OF MY FAMILY

ME

MOMMY

+ MY DOG
BUBU

GRANDPA
+
GRANDMA

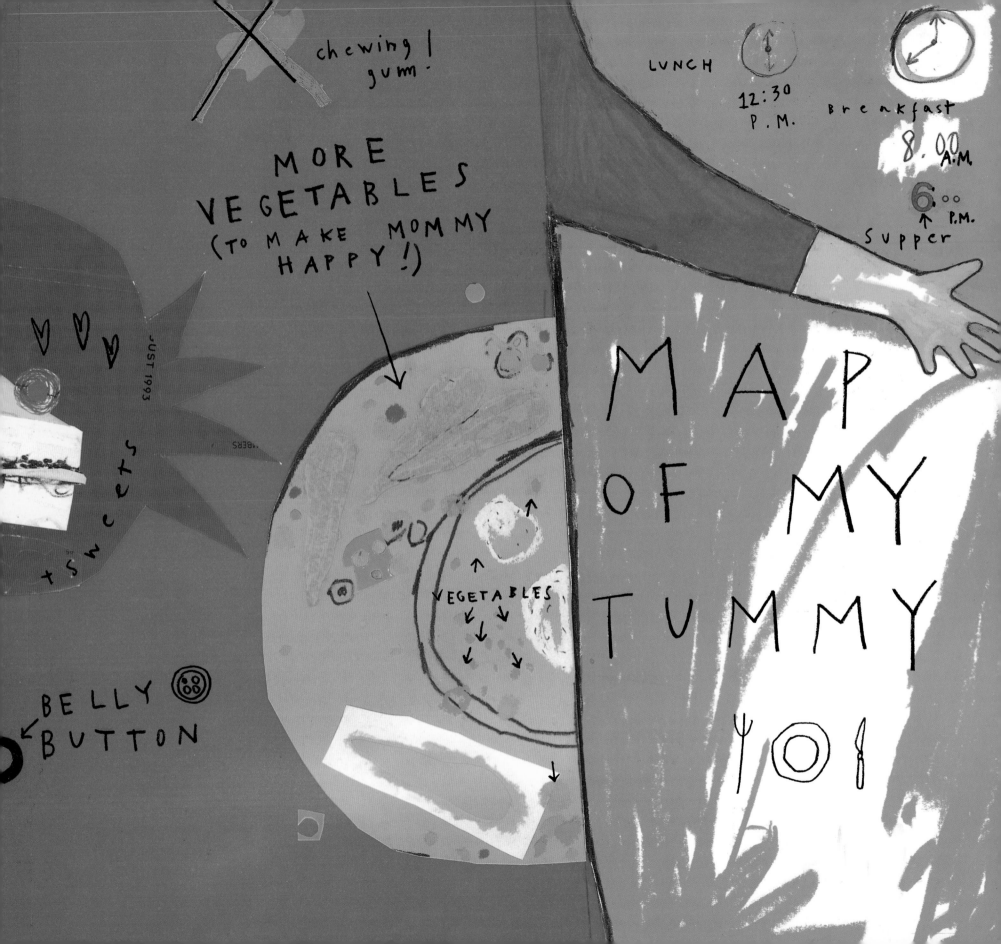

BLUE SKY

VIOLET

BLACK WHITE

RED

GREY

THE COLOR OF CHERRIES!

MAP

PINK

RED + WHITE = (LIKE THE SKY ON A RAINY DAY)

FRIENDS

MOON + STARS ALBERTINA MY

SISTER

BOOKS

MAP OF MY HEART

SUNNY DAYS

CHOCKOLATE

MOMMY + DADDY

GRANDPA + GRANDMA

someone special

NICE SURPRISES!

AUNT YOLANDA
HOLIDAYS
MY FAVORITE
Nº 2
MY TEACHER
TRIPS
MILLI K.
CHRISTMAS
♥ MAPS

FRANCO
SUE!

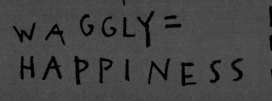

WAGGLY = HAPPINESS

TAIL

MAP OF MY

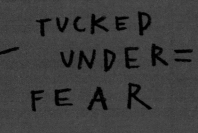

TUCKED UNDER = FEAR

↑ MUD

BUBU

2

1

my name is

DOG
DOG'S DREAM
POINTED EARS = ALERT
3
MUD
4 LEGS
WET NOSE = HEALTHY DOG

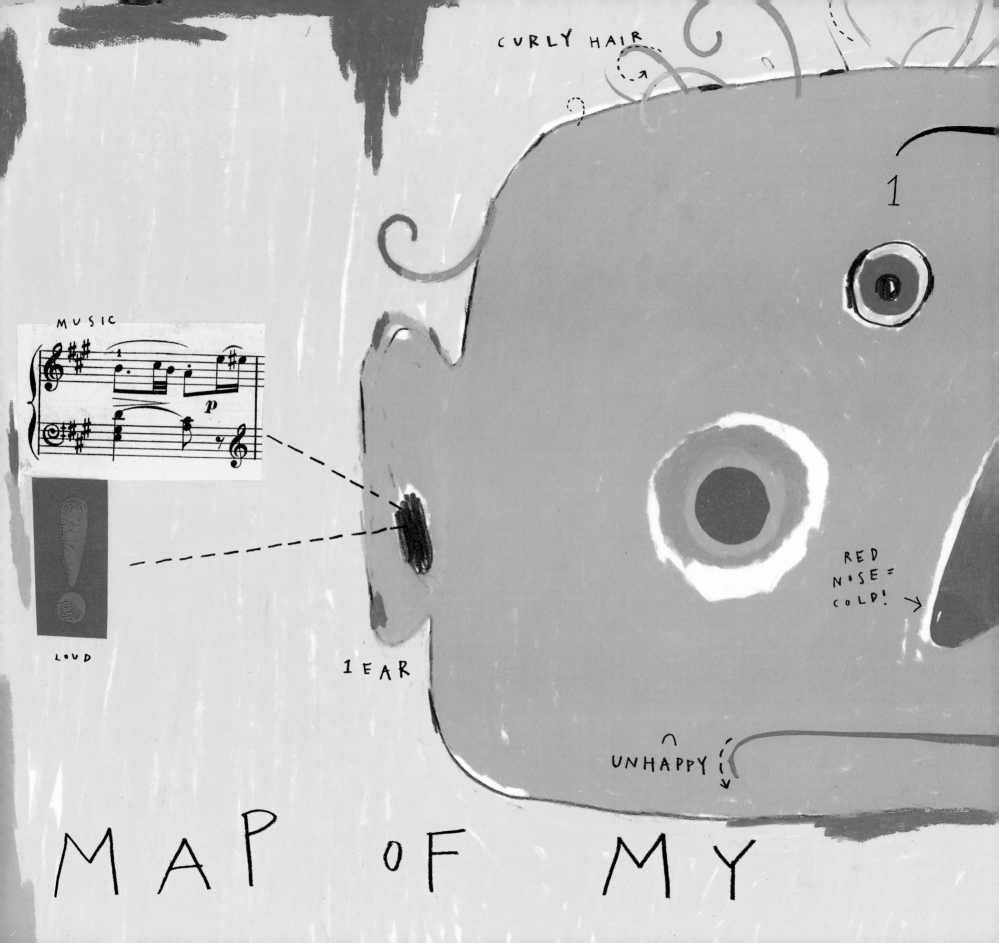

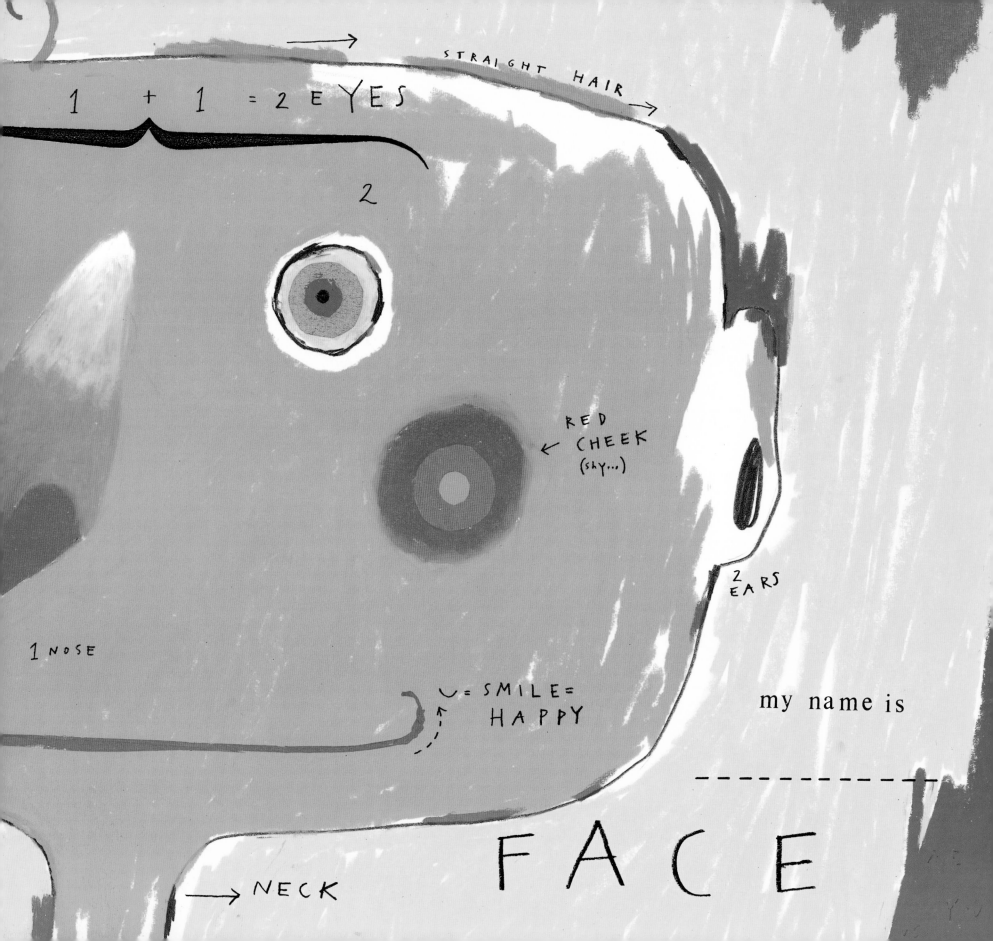

my life jacket

BUOY

BOAT

A SCHOOL OF 6 FISH

SAILBOAT

OF THE SEASIDE

MAPS

W

S